THE KNIGHT'S CROSS SIGNAL PROBLEM

BY

ERNEST BRAMAH

British Library Cataloguing-in-Publication Data
A catalogue record for this book is available from the
British Library

CONTENTS

ERNEST BRAMAH

Ernest Bramah Smith was born was near Manchester in 1868. He was a poor student, and dropped out of the Manchester Grammar School when sixteen years old to go into the farming business. During his late teens, he began to contribute short stories and vignettes to the *Birmingham News*. A few years later, he moved to London's Grub Street - famous for its concentration of impoverished 'hack writers'– and eventually became editor of a number of journals.

Bramah found commercial and critical success with his first novel, *The Wallet of Kai Lung*, in 1900. The character of Kai Lang–a travelling storyteller in China–went on to feature in a number of his works, many of which featured fantasy elements such as dragons and gods, and utilised an idiosyncratic form of Mandarin English. Something of a recluse, Bramah also wrote political science fiction–in fact, his 1907 novel *The Secret of the League* was acknowledged by George Orwell as a forerunner to his famous novel *Nineteen Eighty-Four*–and even tried his hand at detective fiction. At the height of his fame, Bramah's mystery tales, featuring the blind detective Max Carrados, appeared alongside Sir Arthur Conan Doyle's *Sherlock Holmes* stories in the *Strand Magazine*, even occasionally outselling them. Bramah died in 1942, aged 74.

THE KNIGHT'S CROSS SIGNAL PROBLEM

ERNEST BRAMAH

***

'Louis,' exclaimed Mr Carrados, with the air of genial gaiety that Carlyle had found so incongruous to his conception of a blind man, 'you have a mystery somewhere about you! I know it by your step.'

Nearly a month had passed since the incident of the false Dionysius had led to the two men meeting. It was now December. Whatever Mr Carlyle's step might indicate to the inner eye it betokened to the casual observer the manner of a crisp, alert, self-possessed man of business. Carlyle, in truth, betrayed nothing of the pessimism and despondency that had marked him on the earlier occasion.

'You have only yourself to thank that it is a very poor one,' he retorted. 'If you hadn't held me to a hasty promise—'

'To give me an option on the next case that baffled you, no matter what it was—'

'Just so. The consequence is that you get a very unsatisfactory affair that has no special interest to an amateur and is only baffling because it is—well—'

'Well, baffling?'

'Exactly, Max. Your would-be jest has discovered the proverbial truth. I need hardly tell you that it is only the insoluble that is finally baffling and this is very probably insoluble. You remember the awful smash on the Central and Suburban at Knight's Cross station a few weeks ago?'

'Yes,' replied Carrados, with interest. 'I read the whole ghastly details at the time.'

'You read?' exclaimed his friend suspiciously.

'I still use the familiar phrases,' explained Carrados, with a smile. 'As a matter of fact, my secretary reads to me. I mark what I want to hear and when he comes at ten o'clock we clear off the morning papers in no time.'

'And how do you know what to mark?' demanded Mr Carlyle cunningly.

Carrados's right hand, lying idly on the table, moved to a newspaper near. He ran his finger along a column heading, his eyes still turned towards his visitor.

' "The Money Market. Continued from page two. British Railways",' he announced.

'Extraordinary,' murmured Carlyle.

'Not very,' said Carrados. 'If someone dipped a stick in treacle and wrote "Rats" across a marble slab you would

4

probably be able to distinguish what was there, blindfold.'

'Probably,' admitted Mr Carlyle. 'At all events we will not test the experiment.'

'The difference to you of treacle on a marble background is scarcely greater than that of printers' ink on newspaper to me. But anything smaller than pica I do not read with comfort, and below long primer I cannot read at all. Hence the secretary. Now the accident, Louis.'

'The accident: well, you remember all about that. An ordinary Central and Suburban passenger train, non-stop at Knight's Cross, ran past the signal and crashed into a crowded electric train that was just beginning to move out. It was like sending a garden roller down a row of handlights. Two carriages of the electric train were flattened out of existence; the next two were broken up. For the first time on an English railway there was a good standup smash between a heavy steam engine and a train of light cars, and it was "bad for the coo".'

'Twenty-seven killed, forty something injured, eight died since,' commented Carrados.

'That was bad for the Co.,' said Carlyle. 'Well, the main fact was plain enough. The heavy train was in the wrong. But was the engine-driver responsible? He claimed, and he claimed vehemently from the first and he never varied one iota, that he had a "clear" signal–that is to say, the green light, it being dark. The signalman concerned was equally dogged that he never pulled off the signal–that it was at "danger" when the accident happened and that it had been for five minutes before. Obviously, they could not both be right.'

'Why, Louis?' asked Mr Carrados smoothly.

'The signal must either have been up or down–red or green.'

'Did you ever notice the signals on the Great Northern Railway, Louis?'

'Not particularly. Why?'

'One wintery day, about the year when you and I were concerned in being born, the engine driver of a Scotch express received the "clear" from a signal near a little Huntingdon station called Abbots Ripton. He went on and crashed into a goods train and into the thick of the smash a down express mowed its way. Thirteen killed and the usual tale of injured. He was positive that the signal gave him a "clear"; the signalman was equally confident that he had never pulled it off the "danger". Both were right, and yet the signal was in working order. As I said, it was a wintery day; it had been snowing hard and the snow froze and accumulated on the upper edge of the signal arm until its weight bore it down. That is a fact that no fiction writer dare have invented, but to this day every signal on the Great Northern pivots from the centre of the arm instead of from the end, in memory of that snowstorm.'

'That came out at the inquest, I presume?' said Mr Carlyle.

'We have had the Board of Trade inquiry and the inquest here and no explanation is forthcoming. Everything was in perfect order. It rests between the word of the signalman and the word of the engine driver—not a jot of direct evidence either way. Which is right?'

'That is what you are going to find out, Louis?' suggested Carrados.

'It is what I am being paid for finding out,' admitted Mr Carlyle frankly. 'But so far we are just where the inquest left it, and, between ourselves, I candidly can't see an inch in front of my face in the matter.'

'Nor can I,' said the blind man, with a rather wry smile. 'Never mind. The engine driver is your client, of course?'

'Yes,' admitted Carlyle. 'But how the deuce did you know?'

'Let us say that your sympathies are enlisted on his behalf. The jury were inclined to exonerate the signalman, weren't they? What has the company done with your man?'

'Both are suspended. Hutchins, the driver, hears that he may probably be given charge of a lavatory at one of the stations. He is a decent, bluff, short-spoken old chap, with his heart in his work. Just now you'll find him at his worst—bitter and suspicious. The thought of swabbing down a lavatory and taking pennies all day is poisoning him.'

'Naturally. Well, there we have honest Hutchins: taciturn, a little touchy perhaps, grown grey in the service of the company, and manifesting quite a bulldog-like devotion to his favourite 538.'

'Why, that actually was the number of his engine–how do you know it?' demanded Carlyle sharply.

'It was mentioned two or three times at the inquest, Louis,' replied Carrados mildly.

'And you remembered–with no reason to?'

'You can generally trust a blind man's memory; especially if he has taken the trouble to develop it.'

'Then you will remember that Hutchins did not make a very good impression at the time. He was surly and irritable under the ordeal. I want you to see the case from all sides.'

'He called the signalman–Mead–a "lying young dog", across the room, I believe. Now, Mead, what is he like? You have seen him, of course?'

'Yes. He does not impress me favourably. He is glib, ingratiating, and distinctly "greasy". He has a ready answer for everything almost before the question is out of your mouth. He has thought of everything.'

'And now you are going to tell me something, Louis,' said Carrados encouragingly.

Mr Carlyle laughed a little to cover an involuntary movement of surprise.

'There is a suggestive line that was not touched at the inquiries,' he admitted. 'Hutchins has been a saving man all his life, and he has received good wages. Among his class he is regarded as wealthy. I daresay that he has five hundred pounds in the bank. He is a widower with one daughter, a very nice-mannered girl of about twenty. Mead is a young man, and he and the girl are sweethearts–have been informally engaged for some time. But old Hutchins would not hear of it; he seems to have taken a dislike to the signalman from the first and latterly he had forbidden him to come to his house or his daughter to speak to him.'

'Excellent, Louis,' cried Carrados in great delight. 'We shall clear your man in a blaze of red and green lights yet and hang the glib, "greasy" signalman from his own signal-post.'

'It is a significant fact, seriously?'

'It is absolutely convincing.'

'It may have been a slip, a mental lapse on Mead's part which he discovered the moment it was too late, and then, being too cowardly to admit his fault, and having so much at stake, he took care to make detection impossible. It may have been that, but my idea is rather that probably it was neither quite pure accident nor pure design. I can imagine

Mead meanly pluming himself over the fact that the life of this man who stands in his way, and whom he must cordially dislike, lies in his power. I can imagine the idea becoming an obsession as he dwells on it. A dozen times with his hand on the lever he lets his mind explore the possibilities of a moment's defection. Then one day he puts the signal off in sheer bravado–and hastily puts it at danger again. He may have done it once or he may have done it oftener before he was caught in a fatal moment of irresolution. The chances are about even that the engine driver would be killed. In any case he would be disgraced, for it is easier on the face of it to believe that a man might run past a danger signal in absentmindedness, without noticing it, than that a man should pull off a signal and replace it without being conscious of his actions.'

'The fireman was killed. Does your theory involve the certainty of the fireman being killed, Louis?'

'No,' said Carlyle. 'The fireman is a difficulty; but looking at it from Mead's point of view–whether he has been guilty of an error or a crime–it resolves itself into this: First, the fireman may be killed. Second, he may not notice the signal at all. Third, in any case he will loyally corroborate his driver and the good old jury will discount that.'

Carrados smoked thoughtfully, his open, sightless eyes merely appearing to be set in a tranquil gaze across the room.

'It would not be an improbable explanation,' he said presently. 'Ninety-nine men out of a hundred would say: "People do not do these things." But you and I, who have in our different ways studied criminology, know that they sometimes do, or else there would be no curious crimes. What have you done on that line?'

To anyone who could see, Mr Carlyle's expression conveyed an answer.

'You are behind the scenes, Max. What was there for me to do? Still I must do something for my money. Well, I have had a very close inquiry made confidentially among the men. There might be a whisper of one of them knowing more than had come out–a man restrained by friendship, or enmity, or even grade jealousy. Nothing came of that. Then there was the remote chance that some private person had noticed the signal without attaching any importance to it then, one who would be able to identify it still by something associated with the time. I went over the line myself. Opposite the signal the line on one side is shut in by a high blank wall; on the other side are houses, but coming below the butt-end of a scullery the signal does not happen to be visible from any road or from any window.'

'My poor Louis!' said Carrados, in friendly ridicule. 'You were at the end of your tether?'

'I was,' admitted Carlyle. 'And now that you know the sort of job it is I don't suppose that you are keen on wasting your time over it.'

'That would hardly be fair, would it?' said Carrados reasonably. 'No, Louis, I will take over your honest old driver and your greasy young signalman and your fatal signal that cannot be seen from anywhere.'

'But it is an important point for you to remember, Max, that although the signal cannot be seen from the box, if the mechanism had gone wrong, or anyone tampered with the arm, the automatic indicator would at once have told Mead that the green light was showing. Oh, I have gone very thoroughly into the technical points, I assure you.'

'I must do so too,' commented Mr Carrados gravely.

'For that matter, if there is anything you want to know, I dare say that I can tell you,' suggested his visitor. 'It might save your time.'

'True,' acquiesced Carrados. 'I should like to know whether anyone belonging to the houses that bound the line there came of age or got married on the twenty-sixth of November.'

Mr Carlyle looked across curiously at his host.

'I really do not know, Max,' he replied, in his crisp,

precise way. 'What on earth has that got to do with it, may I enquire?'

'The only explanation of the Pont St Lin swing-bridge disaster of '75 was the reflection of a green Bengal light on a cottage window.'

Mr Carlyle smiled his indulgence privately.

'My dear chap, you mustn't let your retentive memory of obscure happenings run away with you,' he remarked wisely. 'In nine cases out of ten the obvious explanation is the true one. The difficulty, as here, lies in proving it. Now, you would like to see these men?'

'I expect so; in any case, I will see Hutchins first.'

'Both live in Holloway. Shall I ask Hutchins to come here to see you–say tomorrow? He is doing nothing.'

'No,' replied Carrados. 'Tomorrow I must call on my brokers and my time may be filled up.'

'Quite right; you mustn't neglect your own affairs for this–experiment,' assented Carlyle.

'Besides, I should prefer to drop in on Hutchins at his own home. Now, Louis, enough of the honest old man for one night. I have a lovely thing by Eumenes that I want to show you. Today is–Tuesday. Come to dinner on Sunday and pour the vials of your ridicule on my want of success.'

'That's an amiable way of putting it,' replied Carlyle. 'All right, I will.'

Two hours later Carrados was again in his study, apparently, for a wonder, sitting idle. Sometimes he smiled to himself, and once or twice he laughed a little, but for the most part his pleasant, impassive face reflected no emotion and he sat with his useless eyes tranquilly fixed on an unseen distance. It was a fantastic caprice of the man to mock his sightlessness by a parade of light, and under the soft brilliance of a dozen electric brackets the room was as bright as day. At length he stood up and rang the bell.

'I suppose Mr Greatorex isn't still here by any chance, Parkinson?' he asked, referring to his secretary.

'I think not, sir, but I will ascertain,' replied the man.

'Never mind. Go to his room and bring me the last two files of *The Times*. Now'—when he returned—'turn to the earliest you have there. The date?'

'November the second.'

'That will do. Find the Money Market; it will be in the Supplement. Now look down the columns until you come to British Railways.'

'I have it, sir.'

'Central and Suburban. Read the closing price and the change.'

'Central and Suburban Ordinary, 66 1/2–67 1/2, fall of an eighth. Preferred Ordinary, 81–81 1/2, no change. Deferred Ordinary 27 1/2–27 3/4, fall of a quarter. That is all, sir.'

'Now take a paper about a week on. Read the Deferred only.'

'27–27 1/4, no change.'

'Another week.'

'29 1/2–30, rise of five-eighths.'

'Another.'

'31 1/2–32 1/2, rise of one.'

'Very good. Now on Tuesday the twenty-seventh November.'

'31 7/8–32 3/4, rise of a half.'

'Yes. The next day.'

'24 1/2–23 1/2, fall of nine.'

'Quite so, Parkinson. There had been an accident, you see.'

'Yes, sir. Very unpleasant accident. Jane knows a person whose sister's young man has a cousin who had his arm torn off in it—torn off at the socket, she says, sir. It seems to bring it home to one, sir.'

'That is all. Stay—in the paper you have, look down the first money column and see if there is any reference to the Central and Suburban.'

'Yes, sir. "City and Suburbans, which after their late depression on the projected extension of the motor bus service, had been steadily creeping up on the abandonment of the scheme, and as a result of their own excellent traffic returns, suffered a heavy slump through the lamentable accident of Thursday night. The Deferred in particular at one time fell eleven points as it was felt that the possible dividend, with which rumour has of late been busy, was now out of the question." '

'Yes; that is all. Now you can take the papers back. And let it be a warning to you, Parkinson, not to invest your savings in speculative railway deferreds.'

'Yes, sir. Thank you, sir, I will endeavour to remember.' He lingered for a moment as he shook the file of papers level. 'I may say, sir, that I have my eye on a small block of cottage property at Acton. But even cottage property scarcely seems safe from legislative depredation now, sir.'

The next day Mr Carrados called on his brokers in the city. It is to be presumed that he got through his private business quicker than he expected, for after leaving Austin Friars he continued his journey to Holloway, where he found Hutchins at home and sitting morosely before his kitchen fire. Rightly assuming that his luxuriant car would involve him in a certain amount of public attention in Klondyke Street, the blind man dismissed it some distance from the house, and walked the rest of the way, guided by the almost imperceptible touch of Parkinson's arm.

'Here is a gentleman to see you, father,' explained Miss Hutchins, who had come to the door. She divined the relative positions of the two visitors at a glance.

'Then why don't you take him into the parlour?' grumbled the ex-driver. His face was a testimonial of hard work and general sobriety but at the moment one might hazard from his voice and manner that he had been drinking earlier in the day.

'I don't think that the gentleman would be impressed by the difference between our parlour and our kitchen,' replied the girl quaintly, 'and it is warmer here.'

'What's the matter with the parlour now?' demanded her father sourly. 'It was good enough for your mother and me. It used to be good enough for you.'

'There is nothing the matter with it, nor with the kitchen either.' She turned impassively to the two who had followed her along the narrow passage. 'Will you go in, sir?'

'I don't want to see no gentleman,' cried Hutchins noisily. 'Unless'–his manner suddenly changed to one of pitiable anxiety–'unless you're from the Company, sir, to–to—'

'No; I have come on Mr Carlyle's behalf,' replied Carrados, walking to a chair as though he moved by a kind of instinct.

Hutchins laughed his wry contempt.

'Mr Carlyle!' he reiterated; 'Mr Carlyle! Fat lot of good he's been. Why don't he *do* something for his money?'

'He has,' replied Carrados, with imperturbable good

humour; 'he has sent me. Now, I want to ask you a few questions.'

'A few questions!' roared the irate man. 'Why, blast it, I have done nothing else but answer questions for a month. I didn't pay Mr Carlyle to ask me questions; I can get enough of that for nixes. Why don't you go and ask Mr Herbert Ananias Mead your few questions–then you might find out something.'

There was a slight movement by the door and Carrados knew that the girl had quietly left the room.

'You saw that, sir?' demanded the father, diverted to a new line of bitterness. 'You saw that girl–my own daughter, that I've worked for all her life?'

'No,' replied Carrados.

'The girl that's just gone out–she's my daughter,' explained Hutchins.

'I know, but I did not see her. I see nothing. I am blind.'

'Blind!' exclaimed the old fellow, sitting up in startled wonderment. 'You mean it, sir? You walk all right and you look at me as if you saw me. You're kidding surely.'

'No,' smiled Carrados. 'It's quite right.'

'Then it's a funny business, sir–you what are blind expecting to find something that those with their eyes couldn't,' ruminated Hutchins sagely.

'There are things that you can't see with your eyes,

Hutchins.'

'Perhaps you are right, sir. Well, what is it you want to know?'

'Light a cigar first,' said the blind man, holding out his case and waiting until the various sounds told him that his host was smoking contentedly. 'The train you were driving at the time of the accident was the six-twenty-seven from Notcliff. It stopped everywhere until it reached Lambeth Bridge, the chief London station of your line. There it became something of an express, and leaving Lambeth Bridge at seven-eleven, should not stop again until it fetched Swanstead on Thames, eleven miles out, at seven-thirty-four. Then it stopped on and off from Swanstead to Ingerfield, the terminus of that branch, which it reached at eight-five.'

Hutchins nodded, and then, remembering, said: 'That's right, sir.'

'That was your business all day–running between Notcliff and Ingerfield?'

'Yes, sir. Three journeys up and three down mostly.'

'With the same stops on all the down journeys?'

'No. The seven-eleven is the only one that does a run from the Bridge to Swanstead. You see, it is just on the close of the evening rush, as they call it. A good many late business gentlemen living at Swanstead use the seven-eleven regular. The other journeys we stop at every station to Lambeth

Bridge, and then here and there beyond.'

'There are, of course, other trains doing exactly the same journey—a service, in fact?'

'Yes, sir. About six.'

'And do any of those—say, during the rush—do any of those run non-stop from Lambeth to Swanstead?'

Hutchins reflected a moment. All the choler and restlessness had melted out of the man's face. He was again the excellent artisan, slow but capable and self-reliant.

'That I couldn't definitely say, sir. Very few short-distance trains pass the junction, but some of those may. A guide would show us in a minute but I haven't got one.'

'Never mind. You said at the inquest that it was no uncommon thing for you to be pulled up at the "stop" signal east of Knight's Cross station. How often would that happen—only with the seven-eleven, mind.'

'Perhaps three times a week; perhaps twice.'

'The accident was on a Thursday. Have you noticed that you were pulled up oftener on a Thursday than on any other day?'

A smile crossed the driver's face at the question.

'You don't happen to live at Swanstead yourself, sir?' he asked in reply.

'No,' admitted Carrados. 'Why?'

'Well, sir, we were *always* pulled up on Thursday; practically always, you may say. It got to be quite a saying among those who used the train regular; they used to look out for it.'

Carrados's sightless eyes had the one quality of concealing emotion supremely. 'Oh,' he commented softly, 'always; and it was quite a saying, was it? And *why* was it always so on Thursday?'

'It had to do with the early closing, I'm told. The suburban traffic was a bit different. By rights we ought to have been set back two minutes for that day, but I suppose it wasn't thought worth while to alter us in the timetable, so we most always had to wait outside Three Deep tunnel for a westbound electric to make good.'

'You were prepared for it then?'

'Yes, sir, I was,' said Hutchins, reddening at some recollection, 'and very down about it was one of the jury over that. But, mayhap once in three months, I did get through even on a Thursday, and it's not for me to question whether things are right or wrong just because they are not what I may expect. The signals are my orders, sir–stop! go on! and it's for me to obey, as you would a general on the field of battle. What would happen otherwise! It was nonsense what they said about going cautious; and the man who started it was a barber who didn't know the difference between a "distance" and a "stop" signal down to the minute they gave their verdict. My orders, sir, given me by that signal, was

"Go right ahead and keep to your running time!" '

Carrados nodded a soothing assent. 'That is all, I think,' he remarked.

'All!' exclaimed Hutchins in surprise. 'Why, sir, you can't have got much idea of it yet.'

'Quite enough. And I know it isn't pleasant for you to be taken along the same ground over and over again.'

The man moved awkwardly in his chair and pulled nervously at his grizzled beard.

'You mustn't take any notice of what I said just now, sir,' he apologised. 'You somehow make me feel that something may come of it; but I've been badgered about and accused and cross-examined from one to another of them these weeks till it's fairly made me bitter against everything. And now they talk of putting me in a lavatory–me that has been with the company for five and forty years and on the footplate thirty-two–a man suspected of running past a danger signal.'

'You have had a rough time, Hutchins; you will have to exercise your patience a little longer yet,' said Carrados sympathetically.

'You think something may come of it, sir? You think you will be able to clear me? Believe me, sir, if you could give me something to look forward to it might save me from—' He pulled himself up and shook his head sorrowfully. 'I've been near it,' he added simply.

Carrados reflected and took his resolution.

'Today is Wednesday. I think you may hope to hear something from your general manager towards the middle of next week.'

'Good God, sir! You really mean that?'

'In the interval show your good sense by behaving reasonably. Keep civilly to yourself and don't talk. Above all'–he nodded towards a quart jug that stood on the table between them, an incident that filled the simple-minded engineer with boundless wonder when he recalled it afterwards–'above all, leave that alone.'

Hutchins snatched up the vessel and brought it crashing down on the hearthstone, his face shining with a set resolution.

'I've done with it, sir. It was the bitterness and despair that drove me to that. Now I can do without it.'

The door was hastily opened and Miss Hutchins looked anxiously from her father to the visitors and back again.

'Oh, whatever is the matter?' she exclaimed. 'I heard a great crash.'

'This gentleman is going to clear me, Meg, my dear,' blurted out the old man irrepressibly. 'And I've done with the drink for ever.'

'Hutchins! Hutchins!' said Carrados warningly.

'My daughter, sir; you wouldn't have her not know?' pleaded

Hutchins, rather crestfallen. 'It won't go any further.'

Carrados laughed quietly to himself as he felt Margaret Hutchins's startled and questioning eyes attempting to read his mind. He shook hands with the engine driver without further comment, however, and walked out into the commonplace little street under Parkinson's unobtrusive guidance.

'Very nice of Miss Hutchins to go into half-mourning, Parkinson,' he remarked as they went along. 'Thoughtful, and yet not ostentatious.'

'Yes, sir,' agreed Parkinson, who had long ceased to wonder at his master's perceptions.

'The Romans, Parkinson, had a saying to the effect that gold carries no smell. That is a pity sometimes. What jewellery did Miss Hutchins wear?'

'Very little, sir. A plain gold brooch representing a merry-thought—the merry-thought of a sparrow, I should say, sir. The only other article was a smooth-backed gun-metal watch, suspended from a gun-metal bow.'

'Nothing showy or expensive, eh?'

'Oh dear no, sir. Quite appropriate for a young person of her position.'

'Just what I should have expected.' He slackened his pace. 'We are passing a hoarding, are we not?'

'Yes, sir.'

'We will stand here a moment. Read me the letter-press of the poster before us.'

'This "Oxo" one, sir?'

'Yes.'

' "Oxo", sir.'

Carrados was convulsed with silent laughter. Parkinson had infinitely more dignity and conceded merely a tolerant recognition of the ludicrous.

'That was a bad shot, Parkinson,' remarked his master when he could speak. 'We will try another.'

For three minutes, with scrupulous conscientiousness on the part of the reader and every appearance of keen interest on the part of the hearer, there were set forth the particulars of a sale by auction of superfluous timber and builders' material.

'That will do,' said Carrados, when the last detail had been reached. 'We can be seen from the door of No. 107 still?'

'Yes, sir.'

'No indication of anyone coming to us from there?'

'No, sir.'

Carrados walked thoughtfully on again. In the Holloway Road they rejoined the waiting motor car. 'Lambeth Bridge station,' was the order the driver received.

From the station the car was sent on home and Parkinson was instructed to take two first-class singles for Richmond, which could be reached by changing at Stafford Road. The 'evening rush' had not yet commenced and they had no difficulty in finding an empty carriage when the train came in.

Parkinson was kept busy that journey describing what he saw at various points between Lambeth Bridge and Knight's Cross. For a quarter of a mile Carrados's demands on the eyes and the memory of his remarkable servant were wide and incessant. Then his questions ceased. They had passed the 'stop' signal, east of Knight's Cross station.

The following afternoon they made the return journey as far as Knight's Cross. This time, however, the surroundings failed to interest Carrados. 'We are going to look at some rooms,' was the information he offered on the subject, and an imperturbable 'Yes, sir' had been the extent of Parkinson's comment on the unusual proceeding. After leaving the station they turned sharply along a road that ran parallel with the line, a dull thoroughfare of substantial, elderly houses that were beginning to sink into decrepitude. Here and there a corner residence displayed the brass plate of a professional occupant, but for the most part they were given up to the various branches of second-rate apartment letting.

'The third house after the one with the flagstaff,' said Carrados.

Parkinson rang the bell, which was answered by a young

servant, who took an early opportunity of assuring them that she was not tidy as it was rather early in the afternoon. She informed Carrados, in reply to his enquiry, that Miss Chubb was at home, and showed them into a melancholy little sitting-room to await her appearance.

'I shall be "almost" blind here, Parkinson,' remarked Carrados, walking about the room. 'It saves explanation.'

'Very good, sir,' replied Parkinson.

Five minutes later, an interval suggesting that Miss Chubb also found it rather early in the afternoon, Carrados was arranging to take rooms for his attendant and himself for the short time that he would be in London, seeing an oculist.

'One bedroom, mine, must face north,' he stipulated. 'It has to do with the light.'

Miss Chubb replied that she quite understood. Some gentlemen, she added, had their requirements, others their fancies. She endeavoured to suit all. The bedroom she had in view from the first *did* face north. She would not have known, only the last gentleman, curiously enough, had made the same request.

'A sufferer like myself?' enquired Carrados affably.

Miss Chubb did not think so. In his case she regarded it merely as a fancy. She had had to turn out of her own room to accommodate him, but if one kept an apartment-house one had to be adaptable; and Mr Ghoosh was certainly very liberal in his ideas.

'Ghoosh? An Indian gentleman, I presume?' hazarded Carrados.

It appeared that Mr Ghoosh was an Indian. Miss Chubb confided that at first she had been rather perturbed at the idea of taking in 'a black man', as she confessed to regarding him. She reiterated, however, that Mr Ghoosh proved to be 'quite the gentleman'. Five minutes of affability put Carrados in full possession of Mr Ghoosh's manner of life and movements—the dates of his arrival and departure, his solitariness and his daily habits.

'This would be the best bedroom,' said Miss Chubb.

It was a fair-sized room on the first floor. The window looked out on to the roof of an outbuilding; beyond, the deep cutting of the railway line. Opposite stood the dead wall that Mr Carlyle had spoken of.

Carrados 'looked' round the room with the discriminating glance that sometimes proved so embarrassing to those who knew him.

'I have to take a little daily exercise,' he remarked, walking to the window and running his hand up the woodwork. 'You will not mind my fixing a "developer" here, Miss Chubb—a few small screws?'

Miss Chubb thought not. Then she was sure not. Finally she ridiculed the idea of minding with scorn.

'If there is width enough,' mused Carrados, spanning the upright critically. 'Do you happen to have a wooden foot-rule convenient?'

'Well, to be sure!' exclaimed Miss Chubb, opening a rapid succession of drawers until she produced the required article. 'When we did out this room after Mr Ghoosh, there was this very ruler among the things that he hadn't thought worth taking. This is what you require, sir?'

'Yes,' replied Carrados, accepting it, 'I think this is exactly what I require.' It was a common new whitewood rule, such as one might buy at any small stationer's for a penny. He carelessly took off the width of the upright, reading the figures with a touch; and then continued to run a finger-tip delicately up and down the edges of the instrument.

'Four and seven-eighths,' was his unspoken conclusion.

'I hope it will do, sir.'

'Admirably,' replied Carrados. 'But I haven't reached the end of my requirements yet, Miss Chubb.'

'No, sir?' said the landlady, feeling that it would be a pleasure to oblige so agreeable a gentleman. 'What else might there be?'

'Although I can see very little I like to have a light, but not any kind of light. Gas I cannot do with. Do you think that you would be able to find me an oil lamp?'

'Certainly, sir. I got out a very nice brass lamp that I have specially for Mr Ghoosh. He read a good deal of an evening and he preferred a lamp.'

'That is very convenient. I suppose it is large enough to burn for a whole evening?'

'Yes, indeed. And very particular he was always to have it filled every day.'

'A lamp without oil is not very useful,' smiled Carrados, following her towards another room, and absentmindedly slipping the foot-rule into his pocket.

Whatever Parkinson thought of the arrangement of going into second-rate apartments in an obscure street it is to be inferred that his devotion to his master was sufficient to overcome his private emotions as a self-respecting 'man'. At all events, as they were approaching the station he asked, and without a trace of feeling, whether there were any orders for him with reference to the proposed migration.

'None, Parkinson,' replied his master. 'We must be satisfied with our present quarters.'

'I beg your pardon, sir,' said Parkinson, with some constraint. 'I understood that you had taken the rooms for a week certain.'

'I am afraid that Miss Chubb will be under the same impression. Unforeseen circumstances will prevent our going, however. Mr Greatorex must write tomorrow, enclosing a cheque, with my regrets, and adding a penny for this ruler which I seem to have brought away with me. It, at least, is something for the money.'

Parkinson may be excused for not attempting to understand the course of events.

'Here is your train coming in, sir,' he merely said.

'We will let it go and wait for another. Is there a signal at either end of the platform?'

'Yes, sir; at the further end.'

'Let us walk towards it. Are there any of the porters or officials about here?'

'No, sir; none.'

'Take this ruler. I want you to go up the steps–there are steps up the signal, by the way?'

'Yes, sir.'

'I want you to measure the glass of the lamp. Do not go up any higher than is necessary, but if you have to stretch be careful not to mark off the measurement with your nail, although the impulse is a natural one. That has been done already.'

Parkinson looked apprehensively around and about. Fortunately the part was a dark and unfrequented spot and everyone else was moving towards the exit at the other end of the platform. Fortunately, also, the signal was not a high one.

'As near as I can judge on the rounded surface, the glass is four and seven-eighths across,' reported Parkinson.

'Thank you,' replied Carrados, returning the measure to his pocket, 'four and seven-eighths is quite near enough. Now we will take the next train back.'

Sunday evening came, and with it Mr Carlyle to The Turrets at the appointed hour. He brought to the situation a mind poised for any eventuality and a trenchant eye. As the time went on and the impenetrable Carrados made no allusion to the case, Carlyle's manner inclined to a waggish commiseration of his host's position. Actually, he said little, but the crisp precision of his voice when the path lay open to a remark of any significance left little to be said.

It was not until they had finished dinner and returned to the library that Carrados gave the slightest hint of anything unusual being in the air. His first indication of coming events was to remove the key from the outside to the inside of the door.

'What are you doing, Max?' demanded Mr Carlyle, his curiosity overcoming the indirect attitude.

'You have been very entertaining, Louis,' replied his friend, 'but Parkinson should be back very soon now and it is as well to be prepared. Do you happen to carry a revolver?'

'Not when I come to dine with you, Max,' replied Carlyle, with all the aplomb he could muster. 'Is it unusual?'

Carrados smiled affectionately at his guest's agile recovery and touched the secret spring of a drawer in an antique bureau by his side. The little hidden receptacle shot smoothly out, disclosing a pair of dull-blued pistols.

'Tonight, at all events, it might be prudent,' he replied, handing one to Carlyle and putting the other into his own pocket. 'Our man may be here at any minute, and we do not know in what temper he will come.'

'Our man!' exclaimed Carlyle, craning forward in excitement. 'Max! you don't mean to say that you have got Mead to admit it?'

'No one has admitted it,' said Carrados. 'And it is not Mead.'

'Not Mead . . . Do you mean that Hutchins—?'

'Neither Mead nor Hutchins. The man who tampered with the signal–for Hutchins was right and a green light *was* exhibited–is a young Indian from Bengal. His name is Drishna and he lives at Swanstead.'

Mr Carlyle stared at his friend between sheer surprise and blank incredulity.

'You really mean this, Carrados?' he said.

'My fatal reputation for humour!' smiled Carrados. 'If I am wrong, Louis, the next hour will expose it.'

'But why–why–why? The colossal villainy, the unparalleled audacity!' Mr Carlyle lost himself among incredulous superlatives and could only stare.

'Chiefly to get himself out of a disastrous speculation,' replied Carrados, answering the question. 'If there was another motive–or at least an incentive–which I suspect, doubtless we shall hear of it.'

'All the same, Max, I don't think that you have treated me quite fairly,' protested Carlyle, getting over his first surprise and passing to a sense of injury. 'Here we are and I know nothing, absolutely nothing, of the whole affair.'

'We both have our ideas of pleasantry, Louis,' replied Carrados genially. 'But I dare say you are right and perhaps there is still time to atone.' In the fewest possible words he outlined the course of his investigations. 'And now you know all that is to be known until Drishna arrives.'

'But will he come?' questioned Carlyle doubtfully. 'He may be suspicious.'

'Yes, he will be suspicious.'

'Then he will not come.'

'On the contrary, Louis, he will come because my letter will make him suspicious. He *is* coming; otherwise Parkinson would have telephoned me at once and we should have had to take other measures.'

'What did you say, Max?' asked Carlyle curiously.

'I wrote that I was anxious to discuss an Indo-Scythian inscription with him, and sent my car in the hope that he would be able to oblige me.'

'But is he interested in Indo-Scythian inscriptions?'

'I haven't the faintest idea,' admitted Carrados, and Mr Carlyle was throwing up his hands in despair when the sound of motor-car wheels softly kissing the gravel surface of the drive outside brought him to his feet.

'By gad, you are right, Max!' he exclaimed, peeping through the curtains. 'There is a man inside.'

'Mr Drishna,' announced Parkinson, a minute later.

The visitor came into the room with leisurely self-possession that might have been real or a desperate assumption. He was a slightly built young man of about twenty-five, with black hair and eyes, a small, carefully trained moustache, and a dark olive skin. His physiognomy was not displeasing, but his expression had a harsh and supercilious tinge. In attire he erred towards the immaculately spruce.

'Mr Carrados?' he said enquiringly.

Carrados, who had risen, bowed slightly without offering his hand.

'This gentleman,' he said, indicating his friend, 'is Mr Carlyle, the celebrated private detective.'

The Indian shot a very sharp glance at the object of this description. Then he sat down.

'You wrote me a letter, Mr Carrados,' he remarked, in English that scarcely betrayed any foreign origin, 'a rather curious letter, I may say. You asked me about an ancient inscription. I know nothing of antiquities; but I thought, as you had sent, that it would be more courteous if I came and explained this to you.'

'That was the object of my letter,' replied Carrados.

'You wished to see me?' said Drishna, unable to stand the ordeal of the silence that Carrados imposed after his remark.

'When you left Miss Chubb's house you left a ruler behind.' One lay on the desk by Carrados and he took it up as he spoke.

'I don't understand what you are talking about,' said Drishna guardedly. 'You are making some mistake.'

'The ruler was marked at four and seven-eighths inches—the measure of the glass of the signal lamp outside.'

The unfortunate young man was unable to repress a start. His face lost its healthy tone. Then, with a sudden impulse, he made a step forward and snatched the object from Carrados's hand.

'If it is mine I have a right to it,' he exclaimed, snapping the ruler in two and throwing it on to the back of the blazing fire. 'It is nothing.'

'Pardon me, I did not say that the one you have so impetuously disposed of was yours. As a matter of fact, it was mine. Yours is—elsewhere.'

'Wherever it is you have no right to it if it is mine,'

panted Drishna, with rising excitement. 'You are a thief, Mr Carrados. I will not stay any longer here.'

He jumped up and turned towards the door. Carlyle made a step forward, but the precaution was unnecessary.

'One moment, Mr Drishna,' interposed Carrados, in his smoothest tones. 'It is a pity, after you have come so far, to leave without hearing of my investigations in the neighbourhood of Shaftesbury Avenue.'

Drishna sat down again.

'As you like,' he muttered. 'It does not interest me.'

'I wanted to obtain a lamp of a certain pattern,' continued Carrados. 'It seemed to me that the simplest explanation would be to say that I wanted it for a motorcar. Naturally I went to Long Acre. At the first shop I said: "Wasn't it here that a friend of mine, an Indian gentleman, recently had a lamp made with a green glass that was nearly five inches across?" No, it was not there but they could make me one. At the next shop the same; at the third, and fourth, and so on. Finally my persistence was rewarded. I found the place where the lamp had been made, and at the cost of ordering another I obtained all the details I wanted. It was news to them, the shopman informed me, that in some parts of India green was the danger colour and therefore tail lamps had to show a green light. The incident made some impression on him and he would be able to identify their customer—who paid in advance and gave no address–among a thousand of his countrymen. Do I succeed in interesting you, Mr Drishna?'

'Do you?' replied Drishna, with a languid yawn. 'Do I look interested?'

'You must make allowance for my unfortunate blindness,' apologised Carrados, with grim irony.

'Blindness!' exclaimed Drishna, dropping his affectation of unconcern as though electrified by the word. 'Do you mean–really blind–that you do not see me?'

'Alas, no,' admitted Carrados.

The Indian withdrew his right hand from his coat pocket and with a tragic gesture flung a heavy revolver down on the table between them.

'I have had you covered all the time, Mr Carrados, and if I had wished to go and you or your friend had raised a hand to stop me, it would have been at the peril of your lives,' he said, in a voice of melancholy triumph. 'But what is the use of defying fate, and who successfully evades his destiny? A month ago I went to see one of our people who reads the future and sought to know the course of certain events. "You need fear no human eye," was the message given to me. Then she added: "But when the sightless sees the unseen, make your peace with Yama." And I thought she spoke of the Great Hereafter!'

'This amounts to an admission of your guilt,' exclaimed Mr Carlyle practically.

'I bow to the decree of fate,' replied Drishna. 'And it is fitting to the universal irony of existence that a blind man should be the instrument. I don't imagine, Mr Carlyle,' he added maliciously, 'that you, with your eyes, would ever have brought that result about.'

'You are a very cold-blooded young scoundrel, sir!' retorted Mr Carlyle. 'Good heavens! Do you realise that you are responsible for the death of scores of innocent men and women?'

'Do *you* realise, Mr Carlyle, that you and your government and your soldiers are responsible for the death of thousands of innocent men and women in my country every day? If England was occupied by the Germans who quartered an army and an administration with their wives and their families and all their expensive paraphernalia on the unfortunate country until the whole nation was reduced to the verge of famine, and the appointment of every new official meant the callous death sentence on a thousand men and women to pay his salary, then if you went to Berlin and wrecked a train you would be hailed a patriot. What Boadicea did and—and Samson, so have I. If they were heroes, so am I.'

'Well, upon my word!' cried the highly scandalised Carlyle, 'what next! Boadicea was a—er—semi-legendary person, whom we may possibly admire at a distance. Personally, I do not profess to express an opinion. But Samson, I would remind you, is a biblical character. Samson was mocked as an enemy. You, I do not doubt, have been entertained as a friend.'

'And haven't I been mocked and despised and sneered at every day of my life here by your supercilious, superior, empty-headed men?' flashed back Drishna, his eyes leaping into malignity and his voice trembling with sudden passion. 'Oh! how I hated them as I passed them in the street and recognised by a thousand petty insults their lordly English contempt for me as an inferior being–a nigger. How I longed with Caligula that a nation had a single neck that I might destroy it at one blow. I loathe you in your complacent hypocrisy, Mr Carlyle, despise and utterly abominate you from an eminence of superiority that you can never even understand.'

'I think we are getting rather away from the point, Mr Drishna,' interposed Carrados, with the impartiality of a judge. 'Unless I am misinformed, you are not so ungallant as to include everyone you have met here in your execration?'

'Ah, no,' admitted Drishna, descending into a quite ingenuous frankness. 'Much as I hate your men I love your women. How is it possible that a nation should be so divided–its men so dull-witted and offensive, its women so quick, sympathetic and capable of appreciating?'

'But a little expensive, too, at times?' suggested Carrados. Drishna sighed heavily.

'Yes; it is incredible. It is the generosity of their large nature. My allowance, though what most of you would call noble, has proved quite inadequate. I was compelled to borrow money and the interest became overwhelming. Bankruptcy was impracticable because I should have then been recalled by my people, and much as I detest England a certain reason made the thought of leaving it unbearable.'

'Connected with the Arcady Theatre?'

'You know? Well, do not let us introduce the lady's name. In order to restore myself I speculated on the Stock Exchange. My credit was good through my father's position and the standing of the firm to which I am attached. I heard on reliable authority, and very early, that the Central and Suburban, and the Deferred especially, was safe to fall heavily, through a motor bus amalgamation that was then a secret. I opened a bear account and sold largely. The shares fell, but only fractionally, and I waited. Then, unfortunately, they began to go up. Adverse forces were at work and rumours were put about. I could not stand the settlement, and in order to carry over an account I was literally compelled to deal temporarily with some securities that were not technically my own property.'

'Embezzlement, sir,' commented Mr Carlyle icily. 'But

what is embezzlement on the top of wholesale murder!'

'That is what it is called. In my case, however, it was only to be temporary. Unfortunately, the rise continued. Then, at the height of my despair, I chanced to be returning to Swanstead rather earlier than usual one evening, and the train was stopped at a certain signal to let another pass. There was conversation in the carriage and I learned certain details. One said that there would be an accident some day, and so forth. In a flash–as by an inspiration–I saw how the circumstance might be turned to account. A bad accident and the shares would certainly fall and my position would be retrieved. I think Mr Carrados has somehow learned the rest.'

'Max,' said Mr Carlyle, with emotion, 'is there any reason why you should not send your man for a police officer and have this monster arrested on his own confession without further delay?'

'Pray do so, Mr Carrados,' acquiesced Drishna. 'I shall certainly be hanged, but the speech I shall prepare will ring from one end of India to the other; my memory will be venerated as that of a martyr; and the emancipation of my motherland will be hastened by my sacrifice.'

'In other words,' commented Carrados, 'there will be disturbances at half-a-dozen disaffected places, a few unfortunate police will be clubbed to death, and possibly worse things may happen. That does not suit us, Mr Drishna.'

'And how do you propose to prevent it?' asked Drishna, with cool assurance.

'It is very unpleasant being hanged on a dark winter morning; very cold, very friendless, very inhuman. The long trial, the solitude and the confinement, the thoughts of the long sleepless night before, the hangman and the pinioning and the noosing of the rope, are apt to prey on the imagination. Only a very stupid man can take hanging easily.'

'What do you want me to do instead, Mr Carrados?' asked Drishna shrewdly.

Carrados's hand closed on the weapon that still lay on the table between them. Without a word he pushed it across.

'I see,' commented Drishna, with a short laugh and a gleaming eye. 'Shoot myself and hush it up to suit your purpose. Withhold my message to save the exposures of a trial, and keep the flame from the torch of insurrectionary freedom.'

'Also,' interposed Carrados mildly, 'to save your worthy people a good deal of shame, and to save the lady who is nameless the unpleasant necessity of relinquishing the house and the income which you have just settled on her. She certainly would not then venerate your memory.'

'What is that?'

'The transaction which you carried through was based on a felony and could not be upheld. The firm you dealt with will go to the courts, and the money, being directly traceable, will be held forfeit as no good consideration passed.'

'Max!' cried Mr Carlyle hotly, 'you are not going to let this scoundrel cheat the gallows after all?'

'The best use you can make of the gallows is to cheat it, Louis,' replied Carrados. 'Have you ever reflected what human beings will think of us a hundred years hence?'

'Oh, of course I'm not really in favour of hanging,' admitted Mr Carlyle.

'Nobody really is. But we go on hanging. Mr Drishna is a dangerous animal who for the sake of pacific animals must cease to exist. Let his barbarous exploit pass into oblivion with him. The disadvantages of spreading it broadcast immeasurably outweigh the benefits.'

'I have considered,' announced Drishna. 'I will do as you wish.'

'Very well,' said Carrados. 'Here is some plain notepaper. You had better write a letter to someone saying that the financial difficulties in which you are involved make life unbearable.'

'But there are no financial difficulties–now.'

'That does not matter in the least. It will be put down

to an hallucination and taken as showing the state of your mind.'

'But what guarantee have we that he will not escape?' whispered Mr Carlyle.

'He cannot escape,' replied Carrados tranquilly. 'His identity is too clear.'

'I have no intention of trying to escape,' put in Drishna, as he wrote. 'You hardly imagine that I have not considered this eventuality, do you?'

'All the same,' murmured the ex-lawyer, 'I should like to have a jury behind me. It is one thing to execute a man morally; it is another to do it almost literally.'

'Is that all right?' asked Drishna, passing across the letter he had written.

Carrados smiled at this tribute to his perception.

'Quite excellent,' he replied courteously. 'There is a train at nine-forty. Will that suit you?'

Drishna nodded and stood up. Mr Carlyle had a very uneasy feeling that he ought to do something but could not suggest to himself what.

The next moment he heard his friend heartily thanking the visitor for the assistance he had been in the matter of the Indo-Scythian inscription, as they walked across the hall together. Then a door closed.

'I believe that there is something positively uncanny

about Max at times,' murmured the perturbed gentleman to himself.

www.ingramcontent.com/pod-product-compliance
Lightning Source LLC
Chambersburg PA
CBHW030530260626
47157CB00005B/1968